About the Author

Brandon Russom is a lover of imagination and creativity. His time spent educating young minds has provided a wealth of experience to draw upon in creating fantastical characters and conflicts. He lives in central Iowa with his wife and their two cats. When he's not gaming or reading, Brandon is dreaming up the next conflict of the next plot for his next story.

Balthazar Bunny and the Quest for the Slicey, Slicey, Cut, Cut

Brandon Russom

Illustrations by S. Dey

Balthazar Bunny and the Quest for the Slicey, Slicey, Cut, Cut

Olympia Publishers
London

www.olympiapublishers.com
OLYMPIA PAPERBACK EDITION

A CIP catalogue record for this title is
available from the British Library.

ISBN: 978-1-78830-430-6

This is a work of fiction.
Names, characters, places and incidents originate from the writer's
imagination. Any resemblance to actual persons, living or dead, is
purely coincidental.

First Published in 2020

Olympia Publishers
60 Cannon Street
London
EC4N 6NP
Printed in Great Britain

Dedication

I want to dedicate this book to my parents, Debra and Michael Russom, for always pushing me to think 'outside the box'.

Acknowledgements

I want to thank my wife, Faris, and my mother-in-law, Faith, for their support and proofreading of the early drafts of the work. Their critiques and suggestions added to the story and made it a success.

Balthazar sat under the oak tree on the grassy hill of Sir Squeaks, the legendary last defender at the battle of Like a Million Catapults. It was peaceful up here. There were no carts and no commotion like there was down in the city. Up here everything was calm. He could almost become one with nature in a place like this. He leaned back on the soft grass. The cool mid-summer breeze lightly brushed against his brown fur and made his greying whiskers twitch. Balthazar closed his eyes and breathed deeply as he stretched out his legs, gently running all four paws through the grass before relaxing. He opened his eyes and gazed up at the drifting clouds through the leaves before almost dozing off. Almost, because as Balthazar began to drift into sleep, he was interrupted by the sound of many heavy footsteps charging up the hill.

Balthazar opened his eyes again as four mailed knights crested the hill and surrounded him. "Good morning, gentlemen, milady," he said with a smile. "What does our king require of us today?"

One of the knights, an otter named Pooka Poka, removed her helmet and walked toward Balthazar. She was slightly taller than him, with light brown fur and dark eyes. Her chainmail glinted in the afternoon sun as she smiled back at Balthazar. "The king requests an audience with the two of us," Pooka said. "Apparently there is a mission of dire importance that needs fulfilling."

Balthazar stood and stretched. "Five carrots says it's something ridiculous," he said. He picked up his knapsack and walked with his companions back down the hill toward the city.

Standing in the Great Hall of Castle Mus, the bastion of the City of Melonhusk, Pooka and Balthazar listened to the shrieking, squeaking voice of their mousey mouse king. "Treason! High treason!" squeaked King Nikoli Noodle. "My family has ruled this kingdom for forty-two mousey mouse generations and in that time not one single creature has seen fit to tell me or my family about Slicey Slicey Cut Cut! This sacred and powerful cheese knife belongs with a sacred and powerful family. My Family!" Balthazar looked around the Great Hall at all those who had gathered for the king's "urgent meeting". The Council of Voles and the Beaver Magistrates were present, as were the captains of the city guard.

As the king continued to rant about treason and dishonor, Balthazar leaned over to Pooka and whispered, "You owe me five carrots."

Nikoli droned on for several minutes, mentioning great wars of the past and something called the Bovine Brethren. Balthazar was only partially listening. He was distracted while admiring the black streaks of fur around Pooka's eyes and how the accents helped make them shine. She had a natural radiant beauty that was impossible for him to ignore. Nikoli's shrill voice snapped Balthazar back from his daydream. "Sir, Lady," he said, "You are the greatest and bravest warriors to ever serve the mighty Kingdom of Melonhusk. I call upon you, Balthazar Bunny, and you, Pooka Poka, to journey to the Temple of the Udder, defeat the Bovine Brethren and return to me this cheese knife, Slicey Slicey Cut Cut, by any means necessary."

Balthazar and Pooka saluted their king and then turned and left the great hall of Castle Mus. They proceeded down the street to the headquarters of the Knights of the Furry Order, an organization which they had created and now presided over. The building was originally the home of Mad-Dog Mossy Moose. Upon her death, the reading of her will revealed that the property was to be bequeathed to the kingdom for "the general defense of the realm". Now it looked less like a house and more like a fortress.

"Between you and me, I think our king is losing it," chuckled Balthazar as they walked down the street.

"Balthazar, don't be ridiculous," replied Pooka. "He lost it the day he found his first grey hair, twelve years ago." They both smiled and continued on toward their headquarters.

Inside the fort, dozens of mice and voles scurried about with scrolls and books, each creature conducting research into a different facet, from botany to metallurgy. Balthazar and Pooka bobbed and weaved through the squirming tide of their rodent comrades and made their way to the inner sanctum which was home to the Library of Infinite Knowledge.

Trisha Tabletennis, an ancient turtle, greeted them from behind her research desk. Her skin was dark, wrinkled and weathered. Her eyes were dim from countless hours of reading and writing in the dimly-lit library. She wore thick bifocals and always seemed to have a smile on her face. "Good morning, young masters. What service might I provide for you today?" she asked, her voice raspy and withered.

"We find ourselves in need of information regarding the Bovine Brethren and the legendary Slicey Slicey Cut Cut," replied Pooka. The old turtle smiled and said, "Ah, yes. I remember tales of such things. One moment please." She finished speaking and then slowly turned and shuffled into the dark warrens of the bookshelves.

Just then, a clumsy young squire named Cody Canis came around the corner with a large stack of books and ran right into Pooka, spilling his books across the floor. Cody's face contorted into an awkward frown as he growled. The display of anger was hardly scarier than a butterfly. The nerdy little wolf had a brain that far outmatched his brawn.

As his books crashed to the floor Cody exclaimed, "Watch out, you fool!" He bent down to pick them up and Pooka knelt down to help him. "You should really watch…" he began to say angrily before he realized who he was talking to.

"Oh, my sweet sassafras!" whimpered Cody. He began to cry and stutter as he spoke. "My lord knights... I... I didn't realize it was you. Please forgive my arrogance and anger." Balthazar chuckled and Pooka smiled as she helped round up the books.

"Sweet child," said Pooka softly, "We are not upset with you. However, I would kindly ask that you exercise restraint with your emotions, especially anger. Remember your training."

"Yes, ma'am," sniffled Cody, "I will." He began to walk away with his books, still sniffling.

"Buck up, young sir," said Balthazar. "Tomorrow is a new day and this day is yet living with opportunities and knowledge waiting to be discovered."

Cody disappeared into the labyrinth of bookshelves as Trisha reappeared, carrying a particularly large volume. She shuffled around to her desk and dropped the brick of a book with a mighty crash.

Trisha opened the book, cleared her throat and began to read, "In the beginning there was darkness. Out of this darkness came the Great Bovine. She created the first of the Bovine bloodline and established a mighty empire based on peace, respect and cheese.

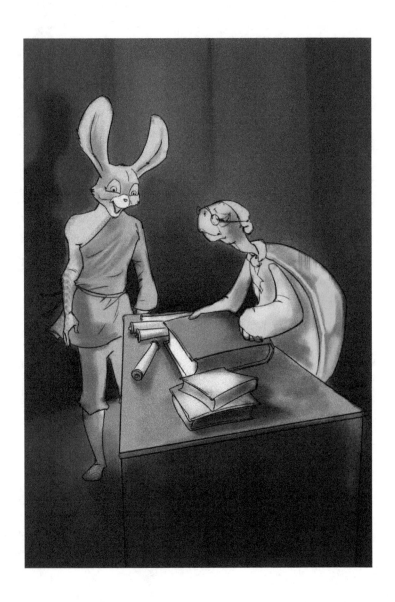

"But jealousy and greed spawned into the realm as some began to accrue more cheese and power than others. The mighty oppressed the weak and justice ceased to exist. Thus began the Dairylord Wars.

"One of these wars was fought for control of a sacred relic, a cheese knife that never dulled and always cut the cheese perfectly. It was last in the possession of Lenny Lactose, Duke of Yogurt. He is said to have sealed the knife within the Pyramid of the Great Bovine herself."

"Trisha," asked Balthazar, "Do you know where this pyramid is located?"

The old turtle wrinkled her forehead and closed her eyes, thinking hard. Finally she opened her eyes and spoke, "I do remember a text referring to a great pyramid in the heart of Big Tree Jungle."

"You mean the Green Grove of Photosynthetic Wonder just beyond the Not So Good, But Not Terribly Bad Badlands?" asked Pooka.

"Precisely," said Trisha, grinning. Pooka and Balthazar thanked Trisha and dashed out of the library and to the supply room where they packed their food, water and sleeping packs. They then went to the armory and retrieved their staves of the Fur Oak. It was a magical wood that was as strong as steel and as light as a feather.

Finally, they entered the training courtyard and selected four up-and-coming apprentices to join them on their journey. Their names were Randy Rodentia, Sally Sue Slimey Snail, Lana Lynx and Feral Phil, a physically fit and friendly frog. By midday the apprentices were packed and the party set out onto their seven-day journey across the Not So Good, But Not Terribly Bad Badlands.

The journey began as a fairly uneventful affair. There were long bouts of walking and hiking by day and stories around the campfire by night. On the third day, the party arrived at a canyon spanned by a rope bridge.

"Ah yes," said Balthazar. "The cliché rickety old bridge. Shall we cross it?" He hardly waited for an answer before setting out across the swinging deathtrap.

"Balthazar, you can't be serious," protested Pooka. "There is nothing rational or logical about using this old bridge."

"Oh, come now, Pooka," called Balthazar over his shoulder. "How else are we supposed to cross this canyon?"

Balthazar began to walk out onto the bridge. "See?" he said. "Everything is perfectly fine. This bridge is as sturdy as—" Balthazar's sentence was cut short as a board snapped under his weight and he fell through the bridge. Phil leapt with his powerful frog legs and caught Balthazar's paw just as he was disappearing beneath the bridge. The force of Phil's landing snapped the other boards Balthazar had just walked over. Randy, Sally Sue and Lana all jumped to aid their comrades. Pooka brought up the rear to complete the long chain of desperate paw-grasping. After many agonizing moments, the group pulled Phil and Balthazar up to safety.

Panting, Pooka crawled over to Balthazar and Phil. Hugging them both she said, "You fools, especially you, Balthazar. I'm so happy you're all right."

"I guess it's safe to say that we're not going to be using this bridge," said Lana.

"I would agree with that statement," answered Sally Sue.

Everyone sat quietly for a moment, catching their breath. "Hey, um… just a thought," said Randy. "Maybe we could try that bridge over there, just past the sign that says, 'Hey, There's A Much Better And Sturdier Bridge Just Down Yonder'."

"Well that's convenient," said Balthazar. "Lead the way, young ones. I've lost the privilege of leading for the rest of the day. Please forgive my arrogance."

The group walked a little further down to the second bridge. It looked far newer and was constructed of stone and large wooden beams. The adventure continued for another four days. There were some hot days, cold nights and questions of who ate the last wonton, causing the group to nearly descend into anarchy. Finally, they arrived at the outskirts of the Green Grove of Photosynthetic Wonder, formerly known as the Big Tree Jungle.

Pooka and Balthazar led their young companions into the underbrush, pushing back the thick vines and branches as they pressed in. There was continuous rustling of the branches above them, following their progress through the trees. Loud screeches echoed through the trees. It was impossible to pinpoint exactly where they were coming from. The apprentices felt fear creep into their thoughts, forcing them to constantly eye the branches above.

"Stand fast, young squires," whispered Pooka. She held her staff at the ready, prepared for an ambush. The jungle floor grew darker and darker as the canopy above grew thicker, blocking the hot noon day sun. It grew uncomfortably cool as they continued to walk. The loud screeches gave way to choruses of "GET OUT!" and "FEAR THE DAIRYLORD!"

The legs of the squires shook intensely with fear, making it harder for them to navigate the entangling web of roots and foliage on the jungle floor. They finally emerged from the thick undergrowth into a small clearing where a bucket of rocks sat on a stump. There were just a few beams of light poking through the trees, highlighting the stump and its bucket. Balthazar gripped his staff tightly and approached the bucket, thinking about possible traps or ambushes that could take place. When he reached the stump he poked the bucket with his staff. A voice rang out through the air.

"Take a rock, turn thrice in hand in order to save your merry band. If you can't, violence shan't be scant, as we descend upon thee. So pick one up. Do as I say and we shall play. Deny my request and you'll be bereft, as the ultimate theft of life takes place within this space, ending your grace without a chase. So grab a rock, my long-eared friend or feel our wrath as we descend." Then there was silence.

Balthazar and the others dropped their bags and held their weapons at the ready, but nothing happened. After a few moments of tense silence, a small gibbon came out of the bushes on the other side of the clearing. It had golden-brown fur with a black face surrounded by a ring of white fur.

It approached Balthazar, holding its long arms above its head, and jammed a long finger into his chest saying, "Dude. You're no fun. You were supposed to run away, scared, with your tails between your legs."

Balthazar smiled at the small gibbon and stepped to the side. He looked at Pooka and the apprentices and nodded. In unison they recited their creed, "We are the Knights of the Furry Order. We do our duty with bravery in our hearts and shy from no challenge. We will pursue excellence, justice and honor for the Order and the Realm."

The gibbon stared at them for a moment and then shrugged his shoulders and said, "Yeah. Cool. So anyway, sorry about the voiceover trick and all that shrieking and junk. It's just what we do for fun around here. My name's Brian Brachiator. What brings you folks to these parts?"

Balthazar explained their quest and Brian agreed to lead them to the pyramid. They walked all afternoon and finally arrived. The great stone structure was overgrown with vegetation and looked less like a building and more like a terraced jungle garden. The stones of the structure were unkempt and aged, devoid of their original grace and beauty.

They entered and proceeded down a long hallway illuminated by several torches. Every square inch of the walls and ceiling was covered with faded mosaics displaying the culture of a long-lost civilization of mighty Bovines. The hallway gave way to a large chamber. Its walls were covered with hieroglyphs of the Dairylords and their greatest accomplishments. At the center of the room was Slicey Slicey Cut Cut, sitting on a pedestal and surrounded by sleeping cows. "Hey guys! What's up!" shouted Brian.

The cows roused themselves and returned his greeting with low energy grunts and moos. Then they turned confused gazes to Balthazar and the rest of the group. "Who are these peeps?" asked one of the cows.

"They're here for the cheese knife thing," answered Brian.

There was a cry of joy from the cows, followed by a tale of woe and sorrow. They explained that after the last Dairylord War, they had been confined to this temple to guard the relic, cursed with undeath until some outside force relieved them of their duty. Now that Balthazar and his group were taking the knife, the Bovine Brethren could free themselves of their bondage and take a much-needed road trip.

Everyone celebrated with ice cream and cheese curds before parting ways, one group heading back to the Kingdom of Melonhusk while the other booked a cruise to the Isle of Endless Grazing, Unless There Is A Drought, Because That Would Kill The Grass, But That Rarely Happens Here. Brian returned to Melonhusk with Balthazar and Pooka. He enlisted in the Knights of the Furry Order and soon after created a class for Jungle Parkour.

Pooka found Balthazar in the meditation room, reading. He rolled the parchment he had been reading as she entered and greeted her with a smile. Pooka gave Balthazar the five carrots he'd won in their wager. The two companions hugged and Balthazar thanked Pooka for helping to save his life. She didn't say anything in response. Instead, she just smiled and squeezed his paw. Then she turned and left the room.

As soon as she was gone, Balthazar's smile vanished. He unrolled the parchment he had been examining and stared again at the few words scrawled across it.

"We have found you, Balthazar, and we haven't forgotten."

Master of Shadows

CPSIA information can be obtained
at www.ICGtesting.com
Printed in the USA
LVHW080759270120
644892LV00011B/532